Lola AND Larch

Fix a Fairy Forest

Sinéad O'Hart

illustrated by Rachel Seago

nosy crow

LOOK OUT FOR

Lola and Larch Save the
Sunshine Spell

Lola and Larch and the
Snow Witch Switch

For Clodagh, star of my heart

S.O.

For Mum and Dad, for … well, everything.
Thank you for being the best
cheerleaders imaginable.

R.S.

First published in the UK in 2024 by Nosy Crow Ltd
Wheat Wharf, 27a Shad Thames,
London, SE1 2XZ, UK

Nosy Crow Eireann Ltd
44 Orchard Grove, Kenmare,
Co Kerry, V93 FY22, Ireland

ISBN: 978 1 80513 102 1

A CIP catalogue record for this book is available from the British Library

Printed and bound in Great Britain by Clays Ltd, Elcograf S.p.A.
following rigorous ethical sourcing standards.

Papers used by Nosy Crow are made from wood grown in sustainable forests.

MIX
Paper | Supporting
responsible forestry
FSC® C018072

3 5 7 9 10 8 6 4 2

www.nosycrow.com

One dark and stormy afternoon a little fairy was flying all by herself…

She dodged raindrops, keeping a tight hold of her larch-cone hat to stop it being gobbled up by the wind. The fierce weather matched her stormy mood.

I never mean to cause trouble, she thought to herself, remembering her mum and dad's disappointed faces, and the neighbours' crossed arms, and King Ash's frown. She sped up, ducking under branches that clapped and shivered in the wind. *Trouble just has a habit of following me around.*

As she dipped beneath a leaf, the fairy saw a dark shape creeping over the forest floor. She flew closer. It looked like a crawling shadow…

"Euphorbia Spurge?" she whispered to herself in fright. "But the bad fairy hasn't been heard from in years…"

A sudden gust of wind caught the fairy and flung her far across the forest. She landed hard and tried to fly again, but her rain-soaked wings wouldn't work.

Panicking and afraid, the fairy closed her
eyes, wiggled her nose and with a *POP*
transformed into a beautiful white rabbit. A
crystal charm, shaped like a raindrop and
shining with rainbow colours, hung from a
pink ribbon round her neck. The rabbit began
to run, fast, but all the trees looked the
same, and the rain was
in her eyes.

The fairy-rabbit spotted a bright light. Could it be magic? Home? She sent a burst of speed through her strong legs and zigzagged through the trees until all at once the light exploded around her. There was a huge noise – and everything went black.

❧ CHAPTER ONE ❧
Runaway Rabbit

"Brr! This is a wicked one!" said Lola's mum as they drove through the storm. The road home from Grandma's house took them deep into the forest. Thunder rattled the dark sky overhead. "You guys all right back there?"

Lola glanced at her little brother, Noah, in his car seat. "Yup!" she called back, even though she was a *tiny* bit scared. She knew it was silly. Mum had explained all about thunder before and how it was just air moving high in the sky. But it was difficult to remember all the science-y

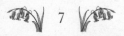

bits when she was feeling wobbly inside.

Mum's wipers flicked left-right, left-right, left-right. It was hard to see out, but Mum knew this road really well. She drove on it every day. She had a big powerful car too – as a forest ranger she had to be able to reach any lost people or injured animals that needed her help – so Lola knew they'd be home soon. She tried to relax, imagining being tucked up in bed.

Then something caught Lola's eye. She looked out of her window, searching the shadowy forest. There it was again – a bright white light in the trees! For a minute she thought it might be lightning, maybe even ball lightning, which she'd read about in her *Big Book of Facts*. She looked more closely. The light was weaving quickly between the tree trunks, and as it went it shone with lots of different colours like a rainbow.

That's not lightning, Lola thought, just as the mysterious light dashed out into the road in

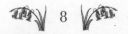

front of them.

"Mum!" Lola shouted.

Mum braked hard and Lola jerked forward against the straps of her seat belt. Noah began to wail.

"Sorry, you two!" Mum called, turning to check on them. "Is everyone OK?"

Lola nodded, and Noah quietened as Mum reached back to hand him his favourite squeaky toy.

"Was that an animal? I need to check," Mum said, looking at Lola. "Can you take care of your brother for a few minutes?" Mum flipped up the hood of her raincoat and opened her door.

Lola watched her mum hurry through the lashing rain and shivered. She peered into the forest but everything was dark. She looked back at Mum. In the glare of the car headlights, Mum bent down and picked something up. Something with long white ears and a tuft of tail.

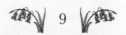

Lola could see the rabbit was wearing a collar. The rabbit's fur was so bright white that it almost glowed in the car's lights. *A rabbit!* Lola loved all animals, but she especially loved rabbits.

"Bunny, bunny!" Noah shouted, pointing out of the window.

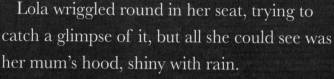

Mum squelched to the back of the car and opened the boot. "There we are," she said, popping the rabbit into an empty animal carrier. "Soon have you good as new."

Lola wriggled round in her seat, trying to catch a glimpse of it, but all she could see was her mum's hood, shiny with rain.

The boot clanged shut, then Mum flung open her door and jumped back into the driving seat, shrugging off her soaking raincoat. "Phew!" she said. "The rabbit's just dazed, I think. We'll check her over at home."

Lightning crackled through the sky as they drove on but Lola didn't feel afraid any more. A fizz of excitement bubbled through her tummy. This beautiful rabbit was coming home with them. And maybe it would stay!

Mum's animal sanctuary was right beside their house. Here she could look after animals in an emergency while they waited for Amy, the local vet, to examine them.

As soon as they arrived home, Mum carried Noah and the rabbit to the sanctuary while Lola ran behind them, huddled against the rain.

"Will she be OK?" Lola asked as Mum placed the rabbit on the examination table.

"She's been very lucky," Mum replied, carefully

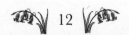

checking the rabbit through its silky white fur.
"She's just shocked. I'll ask Amy to pop round in
the morning to give her a look-over."

"What's that on her collar?" Lola asked.

Attached to it on a silver loop was a raindrop
pendant. It caught the light from the examination
lamp and turned it into hundreds of tiny
rainbows.

"Wow," Lola whispered, thinking of the light
she'd seen among the trees. The white light of the
rabbit's fur and the rainbow light of this crystal…

"What a pretty collar," Mum said. She pulled
her phone from her pocket and took a photo of
the rabbit, who stayed still with her eyes closed.
"And that means whoever this girl is, she has an
owner. We'll have to find out where she came
from and get her back home. I'll put this photo
up around town tomorrow."

"But she came from the forest," Lola said.
"I saw her, Mum."

Mum frowned. "That can't be right. How

could you have seen her?"

"She was shining like lightning," Lola said.
"Like rainbow lightning, moving really fast."

"OK…" Mum frowned, a small smile on her
lips. "I think it's time for bed. For our new rabbit
friend, and for all of us."

"But, Mum—" Lola began.

"Let's talk about it in the morning," Mum said.
"Now, we've got to make our guest comfortable."

Mum let Lola pick the hutch. There were
plenty spare. Mum's sanctuary only had two

animals recovering in it – a squirrel and an owl. The hutch Lola chose had a shaded part for sleeping in and loads of room. They tucked the rabbit into the fresh hay. She kept her eyes closed most of the time, just twitching her little nose as she breathed. Lola stroked her just before Mum closed the hutch. She wasn't glowing now – she was just ordinary white.

I hope you'll be shining again tomorrow, Lola thought. *Then Mum will have to believe me.*

⇒ CHAPTER TWO ⇐
A Fairy Big Secret

The moment Lola woke up the next morning, she threw off her blankets, grabbed her glasses and raced downstairs. The door to Mum's sanctuary was unlocked and she crept through.

"Hello!" she whispered as she drew closer to the rabbit hutch.

But when she reached the hutch she gasped. The rabbit was gone!

The hutch was still locked. Lola looked around the room for a glimpse of sparkling white fur, just in case – but there was no sign of a rabbit.

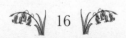

A sound made Lola look back at the hutch.
She pressed her nose right up to the bars and
saw a flash of rainbow-coloured light, which
made her squint. Then something fluttered
towards her face and pinched her right between
her nostrils.

"Ouch!" she cried, going cross-eyed as she
tried to see. Had the rabbit *bitten* her? She tried
to pull her face away, but she was being held
tight. All she could make out were fluttering
wings and a tall pink thing
that looked like
a pinecone.

"Who are
you?" came a
small irritated
voice. "And
– ugh! When
was the last
time you *blew*
this thing?"

"*Pardon?*" Lola said.

"Bogies! All over the place! I mean, it's *ridiculous.*"

The pinching pain in Lola's nose stopped, and she stepped back from the hutch. A small person was standing in it, their arms folded.

The tiny person had hair that looked a lot like moss – it was soft and springy and green. She was wearing the strange pink cone on her head like a hat, and her clothes were made of hundreds of shiny green needles, arranged very neatly so that she could move her long arms and legs, which were thin and pale green like the stems of a plant. Two beautiful sparkling wings shimmered behind her back, shining with the same light as the rainbow pendant that hung from a pink ribbon round her neck.

Lola remembered the light in the forest… And the rabbit's collar… *The rabbit didn't vanish! She'd never been a rabbit to begin with!*

"I *knew* you weren't a rabbit!" she said.

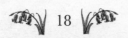

"Of course I'm not!" Larch snorted. "I'm a fairy! A *tree* fairy to be precise. Who told you I was a rabbit?"

"Well, it's just you *looked* like a rabbit last night when we found you," Lola explained. "Mum almost hit you with her car. She's a forest ranger so she brought you back here to look after you."

Larch stared at Lola with her head on one side and one eyebrow raised. "Yeah, I didn't understand a single word of that," she said. "Your mum's a *what*?"

"A forest ranger. She looks after the forest and the animals who live there," Lola said. "And she cares for animals here in the animal sanctuary, a bit like a vet." She saw Larch's confused frown. "Like a doctor, who treats animals."

"I'm not an animal!" Larch replied, fluttering her wings in indignation.

"I know!" Lola said. "I saw you, in the trees, right before you ran out in front of the car."

Larch scrunched her eyes tight. "My head

hurts. I just remember strange lights and a booming roar…" She flopped on to the floor of the hutch, her wings drooping.

"What's your name?" Lola asked gently. "I'm Lola."

The fairy looked up at her. "Larch Mudwort."

"Hi, Larch," Lola said, smiling. She was glad to see that Larch tried to smile back. "It's going to be OK. My mum will help you get better." Lola's grin widened. "And I can't wait to show her that you're really a fairy! I *told* her I'd seen you shining in the trees, and she didn't believe me. But she will now!"

Larch stood up and gripped the bars of the hutch. "No way! You can't tell her. It's forbidden for adult humans to know about fairies. It's the First Rule!"

Lola blinked in confusion. "What's that?"

Larch rolled her eyes and recited: "*Rule the First. Never reveal yourself to an Adult Human Creature, for they are Foolish and Not to be Trusted.*"

"Hey!" said Lola. "My mum's nice!"

Larch shrugged. "Well, you *would* say that, seeing as you're a Child Human Creature." She gave Lola a pitying smile. "But a rule's a rule. I *am* allowed to let human children see me, because they've still got magic in them. Most of you lose it all as you grow up. But if your mum sees me, I'll be in *big* trouble when I get home." She sighed. "If I'm even allowed to go home," she added quietly.

"Where *is* your home?" Lola asked.

Larch looked up at Lola. "I … don't know." She said it so quietly that Lola could barely hear her. "I got lost in the storm."

Lola popped open the hutch, and Larch fluttered up to sit on her hand. She plopped comfortably into Lola's palm, all warm and soft. Holding her felt like holding a little hedgehog.

"It's going to be OK, I promise," Lola said.

Larch pulled up her knees, wrapping her arms round them. "I'm not sure my mum would agree," she said miserably. "She says I'm a menace."

"What's a menace?" Lola asked.

Larch scowled. "Me! My magic always goes wrong. I tried to help our village vegetable patch grow nice and green, but my spell turned it into a mini-jungle, and while I was waiting for my parents and King Ash to decide what my punishment was going to be *this* time, I decided to run away – right into a storm, which I wasn't supposed to be flying in, *especially* not on my own. Everything I do turns into a *total* mess. And as for the rabbit thing..." She shook her head. "Ugh."

"What do you mean 'the rabbit thing'?"

Larch sighed. "I'm not *supposed* to be able to turn into a rabbit," she said. "It only happens because my magic got mixed up with my fairy godmother's when I was born." Larch looked up at Lola. "She did a spell over little baby me, which was supposed to give me the power to 'become whatever I wanted in life'." Larch wiggled her fingers, and Lola guessed that was what casting a spell looked like. "But my own magic decided to get involved, and I got the power to become a rabbit instead."

"But that's a *brilliant* power," Lola said with a laugh. "Isn't it? I wanted to be a lion when I was little. I'd love to be able to become one whenever I liked!"

"It's just that nobody else has a power like mine," Larch replied glumly. "Other fairies are afraid of me. They think my odd magic means I'm a … *bad* fairy." Her wings drooped once again, and Lola felt her heart droop too. She wanted to help Larch feel better.

"Lo-la!" came a sudden call. "Where are you?"

Lola jerked in surprise and Larch fell off her hand, landing with an *oof*. "Sorry!" Lola whispered, as Larch stood up, straightening her hat and giving her a dirty look. "I've got to go to football training."

Larch glowered. "I suppose I'm stuck in here until you're back."

Lola picked Larch up and put her back in the hutch. "Yes, but don't worry. We'll look after you until you're well again, I promise." She locked the hutch door. "I can't believe I have my very own fairy to play with!"

"Pardon?" Larch said, her wings quivering with fury. "*Your* fairy?" She folded her arms in disgust. "The very idea of a *human* thinking *they're* in charge, when there's a fairy around! I can't believe the *cheek*—"

"Sssh!" Lola hissed. "Mum's coming!"

"Lola!" Mum's voice was right behind her, and

25

Lola spun round. She tried to block the hutch so that her mum couldn't see into it. "I've been looking for you, sweetie."

"I – I just –" Lola sputtered, as her mum nudged her gently to one side.

"Oh, there she is," Mum said softly. "You wanted to check on our little friend, hey? That's OK. Amy will pop by while we're out."

As Mum led Lola out of the room, Lola turned to look at the hutch. Larch was back in rabbit mode, bad-temperedly chewing on a lettuce leaf. Her large golden-brown eyes were focused on Lola as her jaws went *nibble-nibble-nibble*.

Lola hurried after Mum. She couldn't help but be excited at the thought of coming home again – to play with an actual *fairy*!

☞ CHAPTER THREE ☜
An (Almost) Great Escape

The moment Lola got home from football practice, she hurried in to visit Larch. "Hi!" she whispered. She opened the hutch and stroked rabbit-Larch gently. "How are you doing?"

Larch gave her a slow rabbity blink before popping into her fairy shape. "Is your mum around?" she whispered, peering out of the hutch.

"No," said Lola. "Grandma's upstairs but Mum's gone out with Noah to stick these up all over town." Lola reached into her pocket and

pulled out a sheet of paper. She unfolded it to show a picture of rabbit-Larch with the word FOUND across the top in large letters. The phone number for Mum's sanctuary was printed along the bottom.

"Mum's looking for your owner," Lola explained. "I've tried to tell her you don't have one, but she thinks I'm just trying to keep you for myself."

Larch's face turned as red as a ripe strawberry. "You tadpole! You can see my pendant as clear as day in this picture. Any fairy who sees this will know that it's really a fairy in disguise – and the only fairy brave enough to come anywhere near a human village and see that poster is Euphorbia Spurge, the baddest fairy in the forest. You'll lead her straight to me!"

Lola felt a flash of irritation. "Euphorbia *who*? My mum knows what she's doing! This is the perfect place for you. We can keep you safe here, OK?"

Larch folded her arms. "Humans always think *they're* in charge, or that they know better. Well, you don't! You're *always* making messes. And remind me who has the magic? Oh yes – *me.*"

"But I can look after you here," Lola said miserably. "And we'd have loads of fun together, wouldn't we?"

"You don't understand. I really need to get home." Larch gulped hard, suddenly nervous. "I saw a strange dark *thing* in the forest last night. I'm worried it's heading for my village."

Lola looked surprised. "What sort of dark thing? Like an animal?"

Larch shook her head. "A shadow on the ground, just creeping."

"Weird," Lola whispered.

"*Really* weird," Larch agreed. "And I think Euphorbia Spurge is behind it."

"OK, you've *got* to tell me who that is," Lola said.

"Euphorbia's the worst fairy of them all," Larch replied. "She *hates* our village and everyone in it."

"Wow," Lola breathed. "Why?"

Larch shrugged. "Maybe because we're happy? We *do* sing a lot of songs," she said, wincing slightly. "Probably a bit loudly sometimes."

"Do you think she's going to do something awful?"

Larch's eyes grew big and worried. "Maybe," she whispered.

"OK," Lola said. "We'll find out what she's up to, and we'll find a way to stop her. But we need to make a proper plan. We'll make a map to your home and find a way to get there, and—"

"There's no time!" Larch shouted. "I have to get home right now!" She leapt into the air and vanished, wings and all, inside her larch-cone hat. The cone dropped to the bottom of the hutch and bounced, before falling to the floor below. When it came to a stop, Larch pushed herself out of the cone and got to her feet.

She pulled a face at Lola as her wings popped free one at a time. Then Larch began to flutter around the room, looking for a way out.

"Larch!" Lola called. "Please! If my mum sees this, we're toast!"

31

But Larch's head was filled with her need to be outside. She looked at the squirrel and the owl, both in hutches while they recovered from injuries, and took a deep breath, closing her eyes tight as she smelled their wildness. She thought of the forest and rose higher.

Her rainbow pendant began to shine,
its magic falling on the hutches.
Their locks popped undone and
their doors swung open. The squirrel
hopped out, chittering. The owl just
hooted irritably.

HOoOOOT

Dreaming of trees, Larch spun higher and faster, until she reached the very top of the room – and then her head went *bonk* on something very hard. It let out a terrifyingly loud "BEEP!" that made Larch's ears ring. Her hat was shoved down over her face and she fell through the air, landing on the floor with a bump.

Larch blinked, feeling dizzy. She scurried across the floor into the shadows beneath a gigantic table and hid behind her mossy hair.

When Larch opened her eyes again, Lola was kneeling beside her. The squirrel was back in her hutch and the owl was safe and content on his perch. The hutch doors were closed and the beeping noise had stopped.

Lola laid her hand on the floor beside Larch so that the fairy could scoot on to her palm.

"You just bumped your head on the fire alarm," Lola said quietly, as she lifted Larch up to her face. "We'll find a way to get you home so you can warn everyone, I promise. And I'll make sure you don't have to live in the hutch any more." She smiled and Larch smiled back. "We can do this. We just have to work together."

"Fine," Larch said with a sigh. Then her eyes twinkled. "But if we're going to work together, can you find me some *proper* food first? I didn't mean to use so much magic, and it's made me hungry. Lettuce is all right for rabbits, but it's no food for a fairy!"

⇒ CHAPTER FOUR ⇐
The Map to Nowhere

In a sunny patch in Lola's garden, Larch lay back on the grass, her tummy stuffed full of primrose petals. "Finally," she said with a sigh, right before she gave a tiny burp.

Lola grinned. "Tasty?"

"*So* tasty. Not as good as fresh snail slime, but it'll do. It's better than lettuce, that's for sure. And hopefully I'll only have to eat it once." She pulled a face and Lola laughed.

"Mum's told me all about the whole rabbit poop-eating thing."

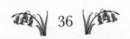

Larch shuddered. "Yuck!" she shrieked, before fluttering up to land on Lola's knee. "OK. Let's talk about how to get me home."

Lola glanced towards the house in case Mum was coming, but the coast was clear. She must still be busy indoors looking after Noah. The forest *whished* gently beyond the garden fence. Larch could stay in fairy mode for now.

Lola opened her notebook. "I've got a plan. We're going to make a map," she told Larch.

The fairy frowned. "A map?"

"Yup! *You're* going to tell me as much as you can remember about your home, and *I'm* going to work out how to get there from here."

Larch's wings fluttered with excitement. "What sort of magic are you going to use to do that?"

Lola shrugged. "We can use the internet, I suppose. I'll have to ask Mum, but I'm sure she'll help."

"Inn-ter-net," Larch said. "I've never heard of

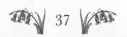

that spell."

Lola laughed. "Come on," she said, readying her pencil. "Let's get started."

"Well." Larch looked awkward. "I'm not supposed to tell humans about where I live, actually. It's another one of the rules."

Lola wrinkled her nose and stared at the fairy. "But how can I help you if we can't figure out where you live?"

"There *are* exceptions, in an emergency," Larch said carefully. "And the human's supposed to have their memory wiped afterwards," she added in a rush. "But let's not worry about that."

"Hey, what?" Lola said. "Memory wiping?"

Larch shrugged. "I don't know the spell for it anyway, so it's probably fine." She cleared her throat. "And this *definitely* counts as an emergency."

"OK, but no wiping, all right?" Lola raised an eyebrow as she flipped to a clean page in her notebook. "I'm still using my memory, thank you very much."

"Right. Cross my wings and hope to crash and all that. No wiping." Larch looked up at Lola expectantly. "So, what do you need to know?"

"Well, when you look out of your bedroom window, what do you see?"

"A branch. Ivy. Usually our pigeon."

Lola wrote this down. "OK… Anything else?"

"The end of the branch? Lots of leaves, like this." Larch wiggled her fingers in the air.

Lola didn't write this down.

"What's outside your front door when you go walking or flying to school or whatever?" she asked.

"*Toadstools*," Larch said, her eyes wide. "Loads of them. And there's a *really* tall tuft of grass just at the end of our street. It's how I know to turn sunwise down to the daisy ring, where my class is."

Lola chewed on the end of the pencil. "Er…"

"What's wrong?"

"It's just there are leaves and branches and toadstools everywhere," Lola said. "It's not helping me make a proper map."

"Oh," said Larch in a small voice. Her wings drooped.

Lola perked up. "Imagine you're *flying* over your village," she said. "Tell me what you'd see."

Larch's heart began to thump. "I've only ever flown that high once," she said. "On the night of the storm." She looked worried, so Lola tried a different question.

"Right. Well, how about anything that's near where you live – something that's big, or at least big enough for humans to know about?"

Larch thought hard. "There's the mountains!" she said triumphantly.

"There aren't any mountains around here," Lola said, shaking her head.

Larch gave her a confused blink. "Humans are so weird," she said. "I've been there loads of times! They're huge, and there's lots of them, all in a circle, and sometimes we go there to have parties or picnics, and one year me and my cousin Cicely made daisy chains to go from one to the other, and—"

"Hang on," Lola said. "They're – in a circle?"

Larch nodded. "A *really* big one."

"Mountains don't *grow* in circles."

Larch pulled a face. "Shows what you know! These ones definitely do."

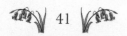

Lola sighed, putting away her notebook. "I
don't think we're getting anywhere. Why don't
we try again later?"

Larch squished her lips tight. "But this is
silly! If I don't make it home, Euphorbia might
destroy my village. And because of your mum's
posters, she might even come after me. I'm not
safe here!"

"I promised I'd look after you, didn't I?"
Lola said. "And I will! You can stay with me all
the time and I won't let any
bad fairies nobble you.
We'll figure something
out about getting
you home. Pinkie
promise." She held
up her littlest finger
and Larch hooked her arm
round it.

"Pinkie promise," said
Larch. "Even if you are a

useless detective!" she added with a grin.

That night Lola found a shoebox under her bed and put some of her old dolly blankets into it for Larch. She popped the shoebox on her bedside table, and Larch fluttered into it, snuggling down happily. Her mum had allowed her to have Larch – or at least the rabbit version – in her room now that Amy the vet had given her the all-clear.

"Ahhh," she said. "This is a lot more comfortable than that smelly hutch." Larch rolled on to her tummy and propped her head up on one hand. "So what's going to happen at school tomorrow? Do we really have to go?"

Lola smiled sleepily. "*I* really have to go, yes," she said. "Do you go to school?"

Larch raised one eyebrow. "Um. School wasn't invented by *humans*, you know. All fairies go to school."

"What's it like?"

Larch sighed. "Boring."

"I mean, what sort of things do you learn? Do you do spelling?"

"Of *course* we do spelling," Larch said. "My favourite one's the Bittertime Blanket, when we gather up leaves in the autumn and use magic and the dewdrops from spiders' webs to stick them together, and it keeps us warm all winter long. That's a great spell."

Lola laughed. "I mean, do you learn how to spell *words*?"

"Oh!" Larch fluttered her wings, blushing. "Yes. And we do maths too. And arts and crafts. We learn knitting with Mrs Araneus. She's a spider, so she's *excellent* at it."

"Who do you sit with?" Lola asked. "Who's your bestie?"

Larch's face fell. "Nobody really sits with me," she said. "I'm sort of the odd one out."

"If I was in your school, I'd sit with you," Lola whispered. She reached out towards the shoebox and Larch took hold of her finger.

As Lola's eyes started to close, she saw Larch's rainbow pendant sparkle just a little, before winking out.

I hope it's supposed to do that, she thought, as she fell asleep.

⇒» CHAPTER FIVE «

School Shenanigans

Lola's teacher, Mr Flynn, stood at the front of the classroom. "Good morning, everyone!" he said. "Let's think about multiples of seven today, OK? Everyone flick to the number squares at the back of your books."

The classroom filled with the sound of rustling. Lola liked working with the number square. It was fun to see all the different patterns you could make. Soon everyone was busy marking out multiples of seven using coloured pencils, as Mr Flynn drew a big number square on the whiteboard.

Suddenly he stopped. He stood up straight and tilted his head, listening hard. "Is someone snoring in here?" He turned round, still holding his whiteboard marker. A giggle went round the classroom and Mr Flynn shushed the children gently.

Everyone looked around but nobody was asleep. Lola's heart started to pound.

"It's coming from Lola's school bag, Mr Flynn," said Eva, who sat right beside the green hook where Lola put her coat and bag every morning. Eva leaned closer just as a super loud snore came out of it. A tiny sparkly cloud puffed out through the slightly open zip.

"It's nothing!" Lola said, jumping to her feet and standing in front of her bag.

She glanced at Hazel, who sat beside her at their desk. Her eyes were wide.

Mr Flynn smiled patiently. "Lola, it's all right. Let me have a look, please."

"No!" Lola cried. "Please just let me wake her up – I mean, turn it off!"

"You know toys aren't allowed in school, Lola," said Mr Flynn.

"It's not a toy," Lola replied.

"Well, what is it?" Mr Flynn put the lid back

on his whiteboard marker and started walking towards them.

Lola's bag began to wriggle and jiggle. Eva and Aisha and Declan and Rob leapt out of their chairs, and someone on the far side of the classroom shouted in fright. Hazel stood up, clapping her hands in excitement.

Mr Flynn gently nudged Lola aside. Her heart went thukka-thukka-thukka-thukka as he pulled open her school bag – and a small white rabbit

flopped out on to his hand. Her nose twitched adorably, her ears looked so strokable and round her neck was her shiny rainbow pendant. Lola sighed with relief.

"Awww!" said everyone at once. Now the whole class was out of their seats, trying to get a closer look.

Mr Flynn placed Larch carefully into Lola's hands. "I think, Lola," Mr Flynn said, "that the rule about not bringing toys to class also extends to animals."

"I'm sorry, Mr Flynn," Lola said. "She must have climbed inside my bag."

Mr Flynn smiled, his eyebrows raised. "Now, let's not frighten the poor thing," he said. "Everyone stay in your seats please, while I speak to Mrs Adeyemi at reception."

The moment Mr Flynn picked up the phone to call reception, turning his back to the class, everyone gathered, whispering, around Lola's desk. Charles went to get his lunchbox from his coat peg and came back with a carrot stick.

"My popo packed my lunch today. She *loves* carrot sticks," he explained, patiently holding it under the rabbit's nose. Finally Larch gave in, rolled her eyes and took a nibble. As she chewed, she glared up at Lola in disgust.

Lola shrugged an apology to the angry fairy just as Mr Flynn hung up the phone. "I've asked Mrs Adeyemi at reception to let your grandma know about the rabbit," he told Lola. "She's on her way now." Lola's cheeks burned red. "I had a pet rabbit when I was little too – I know how lovely they are," Mr Flynn said kindly. "But school isn't the place for them. All right?" Lola nodded, and Mr Flynn looked relieved.

The sound of giggling made Lola look back at the table. Sorcha had taken a lettuce leaf from her sandwich and was flapping it in Larch's face, trying to force her to take a bite.

Larch met Lola's eye and stared at her very deliberately. Her whole body tensed. Then there was a shout.

"*Eeeew!*" shrieked Felix, laughing. "Teacher! The rabbit's *pooped*!"

"Whoops!" Mr Flynn raised his eyebrows at Lola. "Now, there's another reason rabbits don't come to school!"

Mrs Adeyemi smiled at Lola from behind her glass screen. "Your grandma should be here soon," she said. "Is your rabbit ready?"

Lola nodded. She sat with Larch on her lap, feeling glum. The bell for break time rang and Lola sighed. Her tummy rumbled.

Then Lola heard the growl of Grandma's engine and looked out into the school car park. Mrs Adeyemi looked out too, ready to buzz Grandma through the doors. Suddenly Larch stared up at Lola with frightened eyes. Before Lola knew what was happening, Larch had switched to fairy mode!

"No!" Lola whispered. "Grandma's here!"

"I can feel magic!" Larch whispered back. "Somewhere really close. *Strong* magic!"

"*What?*"

"Is everything OK, Lola?" called Mrs Adeyemi.

Lola hid Larch with her coat, pretending to

get her things together. "Yes!" she called.

"Your grandma's on her way in." Mrs Adeyemi pressed the buzzer. "And she has someone with her. An auntie of yours?"

Lola looked out of the door. Grandma was walking towards the school, holding Noah. Another lady was walking beside them. The stranger was short and wide, wearing an odd collection of clothes – purple trousers with a yellow dress on top, and a large fluffy coat with badges round the collar. On her feet were bright-orange flip-flops over thick pink socks, and a hat like a squashed raspberry topped her off.

And round her neck, glinting in the sunlight, was a long necklace with a crystal on it – one that looked a *lot* like Larch's rainbow pendant.

⇒ CHAPTER SIX ⇐

Purple Fog and Power Glitches

Larch changed into her rabbit shape just as the doors opened and Grandma and the strange lady stepped through. Noah squawked happily and Mrs Adeyemi beamed at him.

"Hello, Mrs Adeyemi," Grandma called, and Mrs Adeyemi waved.

Grandma's smile was kind as she walked towards Lola.

Lola stood up, a trembling Larch in her arms. "Grandma—" she began.

"Now, now. We'll have to tell Mum when

she's back, of course, but you're not in trouble with me. She's off dealing with a report of odd-coloured mist somewhere deep in the forest, so she'll probably be too tired to tell you off." Grandma smiled. "And look! This lady here thinks the rabbit is one of hers. She'd just arrived at your house when the school rang, so she came along with me. Wasn't that good luck?"

Lola stared up at the woman. Her eyes were fixed like lasers on Larch – or perhaps on the rainbow pendant on her collar. Then she grinned at Lola.

"It *was* good luck," she said. "That's one o' mine, all right. Escaped during the storm the other night, poor thing!"

Larch shook with fear in Lola's arms. *I can't give her away!* Lola thought desperately. *Come on, think!*

"Oh, Grandma," Lola said, moaning loudly. "I feel sick."

Mrs Adeyemi looked concerned but Grandma raised an eyebrow. "Lola Marguerite Cleary, if you're pulling my leg—"

"I'm not!" Lola said, holding Larch close. "I'm going to throw up. I *am*, Grandma!" She was so nervous that her tummy really *did* feel queasy.

"Right," Grandma huffed. "Let's get you home then. Just hand over the rabbit to Mrs —" Grandma turned to the strange lady – "what did you say your name was?"

"Oh, er. Mrs —" the woman's eyes flicked around the lobby – "Mrs Clock."

Lola glanced in the direction Mrs Clock was looking and, sure enough, the big school clock was there, ticking away the seconds until home time.

"Mrs … *Clock*," Grandma repeated. "That's … unusual."

Mrs Clock sniffed. "An old name," she said. "Very historical."

Grandma turned back to Lola. "Mrs Clock needs her rabbit back, love."

Lola only had one option left. She covered her mouth with her free hand and made the loudest retching noise she could. Grandma and Mrs Clock took a step back, and Mrs Adeyemi gasped. Lola retched again.

"Give me the rabbit, girl!" Mrs Clock snarled, and Grandma stared at her.

"I'm going to take my granddaughter home now," she said loudly, reaching out to tuck Lola beneath her comforting arm. "Mrs Clock, you can collect your rabbit another time."

"What? How *dare*—" Mrs Clock began.

"My grandchildren's welfare is my *top* priority," Grandma said crisply. "When Lola's feeling better – and *only* then – we'll deal with the rabbit situation. Goodbye now."

With that, Grandma – carrying Noah in one arm and ushering Lola and Larch along with the other – strode out of the doors.

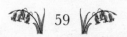

They hurried to Grandma's car. Lola climbed in while Grandma made Noah safe in his car seat, then Grandma planted a kiss on Lola's cheek as she clicked her belt buckle closed. She passed Lola an empty animal carrier and held it steady while Lola placed Larch inside. "Hold on to that rabbit," she whispered. "We'll be home soon."

As Grandma pulled away, Lola looked out of the car window. Mrs Clock – if that was even her real name – stood in the car park looking thunderous. Lola watched Larch through the bars of the carrier. The rabbit hadn't stopped trembling since Mrs Clock had arrived, but the further they travelled from school, the calmer she grew.

"I didn't like that lady," Grandma called as she drove. "Did you?"

"No," Lola replied miserably.

"Are you feeling better?"

"Not really." And Lola meant it. Her tummy was churning.

"Funny bunny," Noah giggled, and Lola smiled at her brother. She looked up and caught Grandma's eye in the mirror.

"Your bunny does seem to be something special," Grandma said. "Maybe she's a hare in disguise. They're magical creatures, you know."

"Are they?" Lola gazed down at Larch.

The rabbit's nose quivered.

"Oh, magic is everywhere," Grandma said. "Don't you think?"

Lola smiled at Larch. "Definitely," she whispered.

Back at Lola's house, Grandma put Noah down for his nap and then settled into a comfy chair in the sunny corner of the kitchen. Soon, she fell into a doze herself.

Lola took rabbit-Larch out to the garden and sat on the grass. She stroked her silky ears. Then Larch's nose wiggled and she switched back to fairy mode.

"Are you OK?" Lola whispered.

"That lady," Larch whispered back, "Mrs Clock. She wasn't a lady at all. That was Euphorbia Spurge!"

Lola's eyes opened wide. "*What?*"

Larch nodded. "She was using a glamour. It's a spell that changes how you look, but only to humans. Fairies can see right through it. They take a *lot* of magic. I told you I could feel it!"

"She wanted to take you away!" Lola said. As she spoke, one of Larch's ears suddenly switched to rabbit mode.

Larch gasped and her ear switched back.

"That was weird," Lola whispered.

Larch looked up at Lola with scared eyes. "*Too* weird."

"So you were right. Euphorbia Spurge has come after you. Right into the human world," Lola said. "Why?"

Larch shrugged. "Maybe she knows I saw the spell she was working on in the forest?"

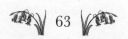

She blinked, trying not to cry. "I have to get home. I want my mum and dad."

Lola noticed a large stately-looking snail making its slow journey up the garden wall. "Hey," she said. "I know what might make you feel better." She held Larch up so she could see the trail of glistening slime marking the snail's journey.

"Oooh," Larch said, brightening.

A few minutes later she was curled on Lola's lap, her tummy bulging, her face and fingers covered in something sticky and shiny. The snail slid on, unaware that handfuls had been taken out of its slime trail by a hungry fairy.

"Happy?" Lola asked.

"Maybe a buttercup or two for afters," said Larch with a quiet burp.

Lola pulled some buttercups for her as Larch sat up. As the fairy ate, she looked thoughtful.

"That emergency your mum's been called to in the forest," Larch said through a mouthful of

yellow, "iss *def'ly* Euphorbia."

"What do you mean? Also, ick. Don't talk with your mouth full."

Larch swallowed. "Sorry," she said. "It's Euphorbia. Got to be. Purple fog is a sure sign of her magic."

"I wonder what she's up to?"

"I've got to get home and warn everyone," Larch said anxiously.

"But we still don't know where to go," Lola said. "We can't just wander into the forest – it's huge. We'll never find your home that way."

"But I'm wasting time here," Larch said, her hands making two tiny fists. "I'm the only one who knows about Euphorbia, and she's trying to stop me from telling. That makes it even more important to get home!"

"But you can't!" Lola pleaded. "Who knows what could happen to you in the forest if you go in without a map? Please, Larch. You have to stay where you're safe."

"This is so silly!" Larch stood up and stamped her foot. "I should be able to do this. I've got *magic –*" at these words her nose and mouth became a rabbit's nose and mouth for a second or two – "but it's starting to go wrong! Maybe because I've been away so long. If it runs out, I don't know what will happen to me. I can't just keep waiting here. What's a fairy without magic?"

❧ CHAPTER SEVEN ❧

A Night-time Rescue

Lola woke with a start, still half wrapped up in the dream she'd been having – a dream where she'd seen a sudden bright rainbow light. She looked at Larch's shoebox bed. It was empty.

"*Larch!*" Lola whispered frantically.

But there was no sign of the fairy. Lola's mind raced. Had Euphorbia Spurge *taken* her? Or had Larch tried to get home alone? The fairy had been really quiet the evening before, and Lola had been able to feel her sadness and worry. Now there was a ball of worry deep in her own tummy. Lola knew she couldn't abandon her friend – but Mum was still out dealing with the strange mist and if Grandma caught her out of bed, and out of *doors*, in the middle of the night, she shuddered at how much trouble she'd be in. Finally, she crept out of bed and padded to the front hallway.

She pulled her wellies off their stand, took her mum's torch from its shelf and grabbed her coat from the rack, and the next thing she knew she was outside – in the darkness *alone*.

She ran across the garden, leapt over the fence and headed for the thickest part of the forest.

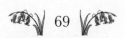

Lola's house was surrounded by trees, and she was used to being among them, but it had been a long while since her last night-time badger-watching excursion with Mum. As she ran, she clicked the torch on. By torchlight the trees looked like they were dancing or wriggling.

"Larch!" she shouted. "*Larch!* Where are you?"

There was no reply. Lola stopped running and tried to get her bearings. All she could hear was her own breath, but then she began to hear another noise – an unexpected and strange one. It was like lots of tiny squeaks, a carpet of chittering, cheeping sounds, and something about it made her uneasy and a little bit scared. She spun on the spot, pointing the beam of the torch at the ground.

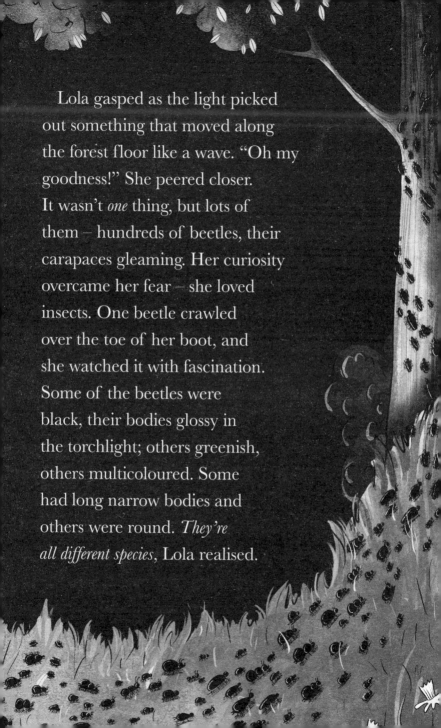

Lola gasped as the light picked
out something that moved along
the forest floor like a wave. "Oh my
goodness!" She peered closer.
It wasn't *one* thing, but lots of
them – hundreds of beetles, their
carapaces gleaming. Her curiosity
overcame her fear – she loved
insects. One beetle crawled
over the toe of her boot, and
she watched it with fascination.
Some of the beetles were
black, their bodies glossy in
the torchlight; others greenish,
others multicoloured. Some
had long narrow bodies and
others were round. *They're
all different species*, Lola realised.

She shone her torch in the direction they were moving, wondering why so many beetles would be swarming and travelling in the same direction – and at night. She picked one up and placed it away from the group. For a moment the insect seemed frozen, then it waggled its antennae and scurried back to join the others, disappearing into the flow.

Lola frowned. *The dark creeping shape*, she thought. *This is what Larch saw on the night of the storm. The beetles are swarming towards her village…*

"Which means," she said aloud, "Euphorbia Spurge is behind it." Lola bent down and whispered to the beetles. "That's why you're acting like this – you're under a spell!"

Lola felt a surge of anger towards Euphorbia Spurge. How *dare* she hold these beetles captive! They were innocent creatures, and Lola knew from her mum's work how many species of beetle were vital for the forest. She spoke to the beetles again. "I'm going to help you, don't worry. I just have to find my friend first."

Carefully, Lola moved away from the stream of beetles and then she ran deeper into the forest. Eventually, through the trees, she saw a ball of rainbow-coloured light.

"Larch!" she cried. She switched off her torch and slid it into her pocket as she ran towards the light. Larch turned to her, dropping out of the air and landing neatly in Lola's outstretched hands. Lola stared at Larch's tiny face.

"I – I'm sorry I didn't listen to you," Larch said. "I couldn't wait any more, and I wanted to get home, but you were right – the forest's just too big. And then I felt Euphorbia's magic, and *look*."

She pointed through the trees at the wave of beetles. "There are *millions* of them."

"I think they're under a spell," Lola said. "It's like they're robots."

Larch nodded. "It's Euphorbia. We *have* to stop her."

Without warning Larch popped from fairy mode to rabbit mode and Lola almost dropped her. Then she turned back into a fairy but her ears remained rabbity. In the next moment she gained a huge tufted rabbit tail.

"What's going on?" Lola cried.

"How am *I* supposed to know?" Larch shouted. Her rainbow light flickered and she looked like she was about to cry. "Just because I'm a fairy doesn't mean I know everything about magic!" Her light flickered one more time and went out.

Plunged into the darkness of the forest, Lola tried to control the fear rising in her chest. Then, a few metres away, she noticed an odd new light. It was purple, and moved like mist seeping between the trunks. The light reached out to pull itself through the forest, as though it had a hundred sticky tentacles. And at the heart of it hovered a fairy, her large wings dark-veined. Round her neck was a luminous purple pendant that swirled with threads of darkness.

Lola's heart dropped. And then Euphorbia Spurge turned and noticed the girl and the fairy. Straight away a tendril of light began to stretch towards them.

"Run!" cried Larch.

Clutching Larch to her chest, Lola spun on the spot and tore through the undergrowth, crashing and snapping and tearing. She ran until she reached her garden fence, leaping over it in a flash and hurrying towards the front door. She flung herself inside and locked the door tight behind her.

Larch gasped. "We're safe. Fairies can't go into a human dwelling place uninvited."

"Well, that's a relief," Lola whispered. Still cradling Larch, she slumped against the wall and slid down it until her bottom met the cold kitchen tiles. She closed her eyes as her heartbeat gradually calmed. Once the sound of rushing blood had stopped thumping in her ears, she opened her eyes. Then she spotted something on the fridge.

A magnet with a photo of a local tourist site on it.

In Lola's arms Larch sat up straighter, quivering like a jelly. Her eyes were focused on

the magnet too – because in the photo was a forest clearing, and in the clearing was a circle of large moss-covered stones.

"The mountains!" said Larch.

"The stone circle!" said Lola at the same time. "So that's where you meant. It's in the forest! I know it. We go for picnics there in the summer."

"I can go home!" Larch cried.

Lola picked her up and kissed her larch-cone hat. "I promise we'll get you there tomorrow, and then we'll stop Euphorbia, whatever it takes."

⟫ CHAPTER EIGHT ⟪
The Forest Quest

"Hello, girls!"

Grandma's voice startled Larch. For a moment she was a rabbit with a fairy head, then a fairy with a rabbit head, then a rabbit with fairy wings, before she managed to get herself the right way round. Lola, with rabbit-Larch in her arms, jerked awake. She remembered curling up on the sofa with Larch the night before, just to rest for a moment, but had they slept here all night?

"Morning, Grandma," Lola murmured,

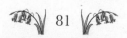

rubbing her eyes as she sat up. Then she remembered her plan.

"Grandma, I have the *best* idea," Lola said brightly. "Why don't we take a picnic to the stone circle today?"

Grandma turned, her eyebrows high. "Fantastic! Today's the spring equinox too – one of those magical turning points of the year. We couldn't pick a better day for it."

Larch vibrated in Lola's arms, her nose twitching even faster. Lola looked down into her excited eyes, wide and bright and full of hope.

Lola helped Grandma put the picnic things together, then made her way towards the door to the animal sanctuary. "Just putting the rabbit into her hutch, Grandma!" she called – but instead she hid in the living-room doorway while Larch popped into fairy-mode. Lola slipped the fairy into the pocket of her rucksack, and then they hurried back to the kitchen.

They left the garden for the forest, Grandma and Lola walking hand in hand. Noah was strapped to Grandma's chest in his cosy baby sling, and she carried the picnic stuff in her rucksack. Hidden in the pocket of Lola's rucksack, Larch munched quietly on a buttercup.

The forest swallowed them up. As soon as they stepped in, the sunshine of the day dwindled to a strange soft light. The trees were steady and comforting, their crowns rustling in the breeze.

Lola breathed in deeply. There was something magical about the air inside a forest.

"Maybe we'll see a deer," she said, as they climbed over a tree root.

"Wouldn't that be lovely?" Grandma agreed. "I hope we see some fairies." She glanced at Lola, her eyes twinkling.

"Fairies?" Lola replied carefully.

"I was sure they were real when I was your age," Grandma said. "I used to leave out treats for them – little offerings, like a saucer of milk or buns. I still do. And, deep down, I still believe in them. Don't you?"

Lola nodded, feeling a buzz of happiness in her chest. "Grandma, you're the best!"

Grandma laughed as they walked on. "I try!"

It was nearly midday when they reached a sunlit clearing in the forest. In the middle was a collection of huge standing stones, some slightly tilted and others proud and tall, all covered with moss and flowers and trails of snail slime.

"The stone circle!" Lola cried, running towards it.

"Don't go inside!" Grandma warned. "That's the fairies' space, not ours. We should respect them. Right?"

Lola stopped short. "I'll just walk around the outside," she said.

Grandma put a blanket on the ground and let Noah out of the sling. Lola made sure Grandma was distracted before lifting Larch gently out of her rucksack.

"I think I can find my way home from here," Larch whispered to Lola. She suddenly flipped into rabbit shape again, then her wings appeared, and the next moment the rabbit was wearing a larch-cone hat. Finally the rabbit disappeared into the hat with a sucking *pop*. A couple of seconds later, a fairy-shaped Larch pushed herself out of the hat, looking dazed. "If I don't get home and recharge my magic really soon, I don't know what will happen to me! Can you carry me? I'm too tired to fly."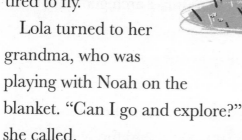

Lola turned to her grandma, who was playing with Noah on the blanket. "Can I go and explore?" she called.

"If I call you, make sure to call back," Grandma warned. "If you don't, I'll be coming to find you."

Lola nodded, keeping Larch hidden behind her back. As soon as they got far enough away, Larch fluttered up to sit on top of her head.

"Left," she said, and Lola turned. "Your other left!" Larch shouted, and Lola spun on the spot.

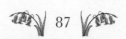

"Now keep going," the fairy said, tugging a tuft of Lola's fringe in excitement.

They ended up in a small grove of trees. Moss grew thickly on the trunks and the branches were lush with green leaves. Lola's eye was caught by bright red and white toadstools set out in circles on the ground. She looked closer. Tiny stones were laid out like village streets, with grass tufts marking the corners. A tangle of overgrown weeds in one corner had a small WARNING! KEEP OUT! MAGICAL MISHAP! sign stuck in it. Larch fluttered down on to Lola's hand. They shared a grin.

Larch cleared her throat. "Hello!" she called. "It's me!"

Nothing happened. The grove was completely silent.

"I've got to tell you something!" Lola shouted. "Euphorbia Spurge is coming. And she has an army of beetles!"

"I *knew* it!" came a tiny, tetchy voice. "She's in

league with that Euphorbia! I've always said it!"

Lola blinked in surprise as a round-bodied fairy came fluttering out of a knoll in a nearby tree, her hat made of whitish-yellow fluff.

"Don't talk rubbish," snapped another voice from the far side of the grove. A fuchsia-hatted fairy popped forth, wagging a finger at the first. "You're too busy gossiping about *me* to gossip about that young Mudwort girl."

"Why, I –" began the white-fluff fairy, flying higher, and suddenly the grove was *filled* with fairies. They popped out of knots and holes and grooves, from behind leaves, out of hiding places so clever that no human eye could have spotted them. They were every imaginable shape, with every imaginable hat, each of them with unique and beautiful wings. Some were wide and wispy, others long and slender, some small and sturdy. Each pair had their own special pattern filled in with beautiful colours. Lola gasped with delight.

"There they are!" Larch squeaked joyfully,

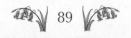

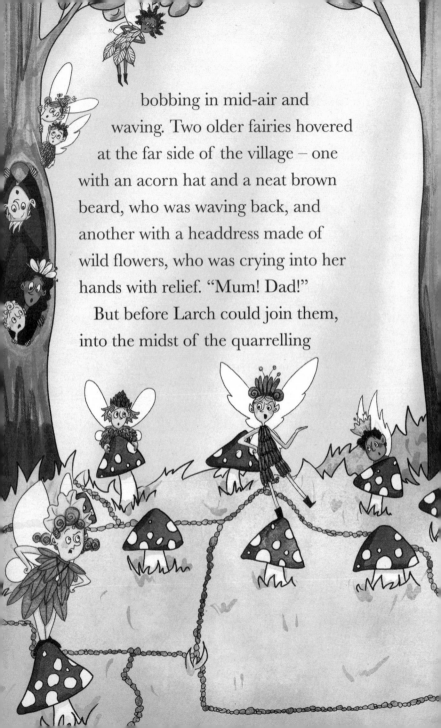

bobbing in mid-air and
waving. Two older fairies hovered
at the far side of the village – one
with an acorn hat and a neat brown
beard, who was waving back, and
another with a headdress made of
wild flowers, who was crying into her
hands with relief. "Mum! Dad!"

But before Larch could join them,
into the midst of the quarrelling

fairies there floated a creature
about the size of a large apple.
His little round wings flapped
so fast they buzzed. He wore a
crown made of long oar-shaped
seed pods neatly arranged
round his head. His beard and
hair were so long that he looked
like a wispy cotton ball.

WARNING
KEEP OUT!
Magical mishap

"*Enough!*" he bellowed.

Instantly the fairies fell silent, nudging one another and pulling faces as they settled down.

Larch gasped, zipping towards the fairy who'd spoken. As she drew near, she came to an abrupt halt, bowing awkwardly. "King Ash!"

"You say Euphorbia is on the march," said the king.

Larch nodded. "Yes," she said. "And she came after me in the human realm."

This caused a ripple to run through the gathered fairies, but one sharp look from King Ash quietened them again. "The human realm?" he repeated, looking at Lola curiously. "And you've found yourself a human, I see. Human child, what is your name?"

"Lola Cleary, Your Majesty," Lola said, wondering if she should bow or curtsy – whatever "curtsy" meant. She'd read it in a book once. Instead she waved.

"Is Larch telling the truth?" he asked. "She

does have rather a reputation for spinning tall tales to get herself out of mischief."

Lola nodded. "Yes, sir. I mean, Your Majesty. She is. I've seen her. Euphorbia's coming. And she has a *lot* of beetles. They're marching through the forest."

King Ash frowned. "How have none of the creatures who guard the forest with us seen this beetle army?"

"The beetles are under her spell," Larch said.

"Maybe your guardians are under it too."

King Ash straightened up, his crown high on his head. "Perhaps she's planning to attack us at the Ostara Festival," he said.

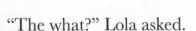

"The what?" Lola asked.

"It's when we have a *brilliant* party," Larch replied with glee.

King Ash sighed.

"Ostara, which humans call the spring equinox," he explained patiently, "is also one of the four points in the year when we renew our fairy magic."

Larch nodded, blushing. "Right. That's the important bit."

More concerned rumblings rose from the fairies, but this time King Ash didn't tell them to be quiet. Instead he turned to his people.

"Are we united? Do we stand against Euphorbia Spurge for now and ever more?"

"Ever more!" chanted the gathered fairies.

"Lola!" came a shout.

Larch and Lola stared at one another.

Grandma!

"You have to go back," Larch said.

"I'm not ready!" Lola said, her lip wobbling.

"You have to," Larch replied, her eyes filling with tears. "If your grandma finds you here, she'll see the fairy village."

Grandma called again, a little louder. "*Lola!*"

"Coming!" Lola called back shakily.

"It's all right," Larch said, smiling at Lola, but Lola could see the sadness behind it. "I'll be fine! You've got to go back to your family. And I've got to go back to mine."

"But ... no! We belong to each other now," Lola said desperately. "I won't –"

The daylight vanished as suddenly as if someone had flicked the sun's "off" switch. Lola gasped as everything around them went shadowy and cold. Cries of dismay and anger rose from the fairies, and Lola heard a strange noise like a trumpet calling troops to battle. She squinted to see King Ash blowing hard through a snail shell, his cheeks round and red with effort.

Larch darted back towards the stone circle.

"Come on!" she called
to Lola as she passed.
Then together they went
back the way they'd come,
stopping short when they
saw what Euphorbia
Spurge had done.

All round the outside of the stone circle, the beetles were arranged in rows. In the time Lola had been with the fairies, the beetles had eaten all the plants in the glade and turned it empty and brown. The beetles waited for instructions, their antennae waggling gently, their carapaces gleaming in the light cast by Euphorbia Spurge, who hovered in the middle of the stone circle, her horrible purple glow like a bruise in the air.

And underneath her, caught in a bubble of darkness at the heart of the stone circle, looking like they were fast asleep, were Grandma and Noah.

⇒ CHAPTER NINE ⇐
Battle at the Stone Circle

"Let them go!" Lola shouted, taking an angry step towards the stone circle. A wave of Euphorbia Spurge's magic pushed her back.

"I have no interest in them," said Euphorbia Spurge in a voice Lola recognised.

She and Larch looked at one another. Larch was right! Mrs Clock *had* been Euphorbia in disguise.

"I'm just keeping them quiet for a while, until I've taken what I came here for."

"You will leave this place!" bellowed King

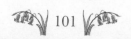

Ash. Lola and Larch turned to see him behind them, armed with a wand made from a length of twig.

"I think not," Euphorbia snapped back. Then she called a command in a squeaking, clattering language – and the next thing Lola knew she was standing in the middle of a sea of beetles, which flowed over her boots like a shining dark river. From all around she heard a cry of dismay as the beetles marched towards the fairy village, their mandibles clicking. "If you want so much as a blade of grass left here, you'll surrender your power to me. If you choose to fight? Well." Euphorbia paused, looking smug. "We'll see what my hungry beetles leave behind."

King Ash turned to his people, who were hovering behind him. Each fairy face was covered with worry and confusion, and several frightened glances were cast back in the direction of the fairy village.

"My friends," called the king, "protect your

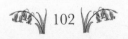

homes as best you can."

Hesitantly at first, and then in a rush, the fairies began to fly back towards their village, trying to reach it before the beetles. Finally, the only ones left facing Euphorbia Spurge were Lola, Larch and her parents, and King Ash.

From inside the stone circle, Euphorbia Spurge laughed. "There's nothing you can do. You won't attack me for fear of harming these innocent *humans*." Her face twisted in disgust as she spoke. "You don't have the power to stop me. And when the midday sun comes I'll be the only fairy inside the circle – which means I'll be the only fairy who'll receive all the magic that it can provide. Once I've soaked up everything that should have been yours –" Euphorbia looked triumphant as she turned to Larch – "I can finally take *your* magic – magic you don't even want. Magic you *complain* about. You've been given the greatest of all magical gifts and you don't even appreciate it!" Euphorbia's eyes sparked dangerously. "You've never unlocked the full potential of your magic, Larch Mudwort, but once I'm the most powerful fairy in these woods, you can be certain that *I* will."

Larch's eyes opened wide. "So that's why you came after me in the human world."

"Glamours are weak," Euphorbia said, shrugging. "I want the power to change my shape – to *truly* become whatever I want – so that I can blend in to the human world. Who knows what mischief I could work!" Euphorbia's smile grew nasty. "I'm doing you a favour, aren't I? Taking away a power you didn't even want in the first place."

King Ash puffed himself up until he was rounder than ever. "I should *never* have allowed you to stay in this forest, Euphorbia," he said.

"You couldn't banish me then, not even with your disgusting *singing*, and you can't banish me now," Euphorbia replied. "But very soon *I* will banish *you*!"

"*Stop!*" Larch cried, zipping into the space between them. "There has to be a better way." She turned to King Ash. "Sometimes fairies tell *me* I'm odd, or strange, or wrong. I've been told 'you'll end up like Euphorbia Spurge!' my whole life, as though it were the worst possible thing. Whoops!" She switched to rabbit mode, dropping out of the air, before popping back to fairy shape before she hit the ground.

"But it's *not* wrong to be different," she continued, as she flew back up into position. "If I weren't different, I would never have met Lola or had any adventures. Being different is a good thing! A fairy can't help who they are, or how their magic works, or what sort of life they want to live. And we all have to live together." She turned to Euphorbia Spurge. "Can't we find a way for you to get what you want – some more magic and a little more peace and quiet? And for the rest of us to live without having to be afraid of you?"

Euphorbia folded her arms. "I *want* you to be afraid of me," she said coldly, and her magic began to swirl around her, growing brighter and more frightening with every moment – until a bolt of power was ready to fly right towards Larch's parents.

Without thinking, Lola leapt in front of the magical blast – but before it could hit her Larch pulled together every last bit of her power. Her rainbow pendant shone brighter than ever before, and with a yell she switched to rabbit mode. She dropped to the ground and bounced high into the air, spinning fast and aiming her super-strong back legs at Euphorbia.

Larch kicked the wicked fairy so hard that her spell shattered into shards – and Euphorbia flew wings over heels into the forest, wailing all the way. Eventually the sound of her voice faded and all was still.

Lola watched as the beetles streamed away from the fairy village, through the stone circle and back towards the forest and their homes. The spell that had kept them under Euphorbia's control was over. She cheered as she watched them scuttle away, free creatures once again.

"To the circle!" called King Ash. The fairies formed a ring round it, their pendants glowing as magic leapt from one to the next.

Lola hurried to the stone circle, pausing to collect a dazed Larch from where she'd landed, in fairy form once more. Lola kissed the fairy's prickly hat as she ran.

As she reached Grandma and Noah, a gentle dome of light formed around them and they began to rise.

"They shall be safe while our magic is renewed," declared King Ash as the sleeping pair floated out of the stone circle and down on to their picnic blanket. The magic stayed in place, keeping them protected and peacefully asleep.

As she stared at her sleeping grandma, music reached Lola's ears. She looked round in amazement to see a fairy orchestra on top of one of the stones, their instruments made from nutshells and seed pods and grass, stones and feathers and twigs. There was even a harp strung with a cobweb, and a drum made from an acorn cup with a leaf stretched over it.

With a loud *whumpf* a bonfire roared to life in the middle of the circle, burning with green flames. Fairies danced in a conga line through the centre of the stone circle, carrying large wooden bowls filled with sparkling silver goo. Others had trays of heaped yellow buttercup petals, and ten fairies carried a huge cake

decorated with snail shells.

Lola felt the widest grin ever on her face. "This is incredible!" she called, holding Larch up.

Larch grinned. "It's the Ostara Festival!" she shouted into her ear. "And we're just in time!"

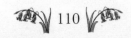

⇒ CHAPTER TEN ⇐
The Ostara Festival

As the midday sun shone into the fairy circle, the music paused. Then, whispering with excitement, the fairies readied themselves. Lola watched as glittering magic started falling from the sky, raining down like shimmering snow, and each fairy rose slowly into the air. Their wings sparkled and their pendants shone brightly as the magic inside them was refilled.

King Ash lifted his wand and a magical breeze whirled around the forest, repairing the damage caused by Euphorbia Spurge and her beetles.

The trees seemed to breathe a sigh of relief, and then the magic faded away.

Larch turned to Lola, her eyes sad. "Now what?"

Lola shrugged. "I've got to go home," she whispered, as Larch came to sit on her palm.

"I really wish you could stay," Larch said miserably. "This isn't how it's supposed to work when you've got a human." Her wings drooped. "We're supposed to be together *all* the time."

The sound of a throat being politely cleared made them both jump. Lola looked round and, sure enough, there was King Ash, floating grandly into view. Beside him, looking worried, were Larch's parents.

Larch flew to join them. Quietly, the other fairies gathered round in curious whispering clusters.

"The ceremonies are complete and our magic has been replenished for another season," King Ash declared. "So, now we can deal with our *other* problem."

Lola swallowed nervously.

"We have among us a young fairy who broke the rules," King Ash said, his arms behind his back. He hovered back and forth in front of Larch and her family. "A young fairy who has, to put it delicately, been trouble for quite some time."

"Hey!" Larch began. "I didn't—"

"*And* if you let me finish," King Ash continued, "a young fairy who has always been *different*. Being different has never been valued in this clan. But –" King Ash paused, hovering before Larch – "sometimes values change."

"What?" Larch said, frowning.

"Larch!" her mother hissed, elbowing her. "You can't say 'what' to the king!"

Larch scowled, rubbing her side.

The king smiled fondly at her. "I have never seen a fairy act with such courage, Larch Mudwort. You came to warn us, and you

faced Euphorbia with bravery much bigger than yourself." His smile faded. "However, for bringing humans into our realm, there must be a punishment."

A chorus of disagreement rose from the fairies all around. "That's not fair!" trilled one with speckled wings.

"She *saved* us!" shouted another, a large fairy with a conker hat.

"She's odder than a three-eyed toad, but she's one of us!" roared a third, which was greeted by a rousing cheer.

"Please, Your Majesty," Lola said.

King Ash turned to her, his eyebrows high.

"Larch got *lost* – she didn't run away. And if it weren't for her, Euphorbia Spurge would have *won*."

King Ash gestured towards the vegetable patch. "There's still the matter of this reckless magic."

"Well, how about this?" Lola said, as Larch

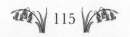

swooped over to sit on her head. "Larch can come and live with me! Some of the time anyway. She can stay in rabbit mode when other humans are around, but she can be her fairy self when it's just me."

Larch's eyes brightened. "I could come home whenever I want to! To see Mum and Dad, and to make sure my magic gets renewed in time." She glanced at the vegetable patch, which was oozing unpleasantly, and gave an embarrassed cough. "Sort out my messes, fix my mistakes, that sort of thing. But most of the time I'll be out of your hair."

"Oh, Oakheart," said Larch's mum, Posy, to her husband. "We could go to visit Larch too. Imagine, a holiday among humans!" Her wings fluttered with excitement, as Larch's dad rolled his eyes.

Murmurs rose but King Ash's moustache twitched – Lola thought he might be smiling. "An excellent solution," he said, and the

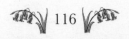

murmuring stopped. "Larch, you are certainly unique – and that's something to be celebrated. Never again will anyone in this fairy clan treat you unkindly just because you're different."

The fairies all cheered.

Larch flew back to her parents, who hugged her tightly. Her mother beamed with relief and happiness, and her father looked proud. Larch's smile was wide.

The fairies' chatter hushed when, from somewhere close by, a strange tinkling filled the air. They gasped, clutching one another in horror. "It's Euphorbia!" one shrieked. "She's back!" They began to fly around in panic.

But Lola recognised the sound. Grandma's mobile phone!

"Don't worry!" she told the fairies, getting to her feet and jumping out of the stone circle. Larch flew behind her. They reached the picnic blanket just as Grandma and Noah awoke. The fairy-magic dome popped as Grandma sat up,

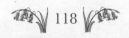

Noah safe in her
arms. Grandma
patted at her
pockets until
she found
her phone,
switching it to
speaker mode
as she answered
it. "Hello?"

"Mum?" came Lola's
mum's voice from the phone's speaker. "Where
are you all?"

"Oh, we came up to the stone circle to have
a picnic, but we must've dozed off," Grandma
said, looking around.

"Silly billies," Lola's mum said, laughing.
"Well, I'm home now. We couldn't track the
mist down. It seemed to keep moving, and
then just now it vanished! Gone, like it was
never there."

"OK, love," Grandma said. "That's good news. We'll see you soon."

"Hi, Mum!" Lola called to the phone.

"Hi, sweetheart!" her mum replied. "Don't give Grandma any trouble, all right?"

"This one, giving trouble?" Grandma said incredulously. She gave Lola a big wink, and Lola grinned back at her.

"Mum, have you had any calls? About the rabbit?" Lola asked.

"Well, no, now that you mention it," her mum replied. "Why do you ask?"

"Because… Can I please keep her? Can she be my fa… I mean, my *rabbit*, until someone claims her?"

Lola's mum sighed. "I suppose there's no harm in it," she said.

Lola beamed. "Thank you! I'm going to call her Larch."

"That's a wonderful name," Mum said. "I'll see you at home soon. Love you all!" Mum blew

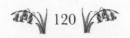

kisses and then she hung up. Grandma stuffed the phone back into her pocket.

"Well," Grandma said, jiggling Noah on one knee, "that was a bit of a let-down, wasn't it? Sorry for dozing off!"

"Don't worry, Grandma," Lola said, turning to hide the fact she was helping Larch back into the pocket of her rucksack. "I still had a *magical* time."

Larch rolled her eyes, and Lola tried very hard not to laugh.

The stone circle seemed empty now, but Lola knew it was anything but. Larch gave a goodbye wave from her pocket. "We'll come back soon," Lola whispered towards the stones, knowing Larch's mum and dad would hear her.

"Right then," Grandma said, pulling out their picnic things. "We should eat up and then get home. I brought pancakes! Who wants extra syrup?"

"I'll take mine with snail slime," Larch murmured.

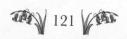

"With *what*?" Grandma said, giving Lola a strange look as she dished out the pancakes.

Lola stifled a giggle and gave a secret smile to her amazing new friend, who winked and stuck out her tongue in return. Lola wondered, with a flutter in her tummy, what adventure they would have next.

"Never mind," she said, as Grandma handed her the syrup bottle. "I guess I'm just away with the fairies!"